Daniel Can DANCE

by Delphine Finnegan
poses and layouts by Jason Fruchter

Ready-to-Read

SIMON SPOTLIGHT
New York London Toronto Sydney New Delhi

Here is a list of all the words you will find in this book. Sound them out before you begin reading the story.

Names:

Daniel

Margaret

SIMON SPOTLIGHT

An imprint of Simon & Schuster Children's Publishing Division • 1230 Avenue of the Americas, New York, New York 10020 • This Simon Spotlight edition December 2018 • SIMON SPOTLIGHT, READY-TO-READ, and colophon are registered trademarks of Simon & Schuster, Inc. For information about special discounts for bulk purchases, please contact Simon & Schuster Special Sales at 1-866-506-1949 or business@simonandschuster.com. Manufactured in the United States of America 1118 LAK • 2 4 6 8 10 9 7 5 3 1 • ISBN 978-1-5344-3041-9 (hc) ISBN 978-1-5344-3040-2 (pbk) ISBN 978-1-5344-3042-6 (eBook)

Word family:

"-ap" → clap snap tap

Sight words:

and	can	down	go	help
her	his	move	the	to
turn	up	with	you	

Bonus words:

dance	fingers	foot
hands	music	

Ready to go? Happy reading!

Don't miss the questions about the story on the last page of this book.

Can Daniel dance?

Daniel can go up.

Daniel can go down.

Daniel can clap
his hands.

Daniel can tap
his foot.

Daniel can snap
his fingers.

Daniel can turn.

Daniel can move
to the music.

Daniel can dance!

Can Margaret dance with Daniel?

Daniel can help.
Margaret can go up.

Margaret can go down.

Can Margaret
clap her hands?

Margaret can clap her hands!

Can Margaret tap her foot?

Margaret can
tap her foot!

Daniel can help
Margaret turn.

Margaret can move to the music.

Margaret can dance!

Can you [illegible]ce with
Daniel a[illegible]argaret?

Now that you have read the story, can you answer these questions?

1. What body part does Daniel tap?

2. How does Daniel help Margaret?

3. In this story you read the rhyming words "clap," "snap," and "tap." Can you think of other words that rhyme with "clap," "snap," and "tap"?

Great job!

You are a reading star!